# WILLIE
# THE
# SQUOWSE

# TED ALLAN

Weekly Reader Books presents

# WILLIE
# THE
# SQUOWSE

Illustrated by
QUENTIN BLAKE

HASTINGS HOUSE ● PUBLISHERS
New York 10016

This book is a presentation of
**Weekly Reader Books.**

Weekly Reader Books offers
book clubs for children from
preschool through junior high school.
All quality hardcover books are selected
by a distinguished Weekly Reader Selection Board.

For further information write to:
**Weekly Reader Books**
1250 Fairwood Ave.
Columbus, Ohio 43216

First published in the United States of America 1978
by Hastings House, Publishers.

*Willie the Squowse* was a prize-winning entry in *The Times* Children's Story Competition and was first published in *The Times Saturday Review* in 1973; subsequently it was included in *The Times Anthology of Children's Stories*, Jonathan Cape, 1974.

Library of Congress Cataloging in Publication Data
Allan, Ted.      Willie the squowse.
SUMMARY: Son of a squirrel and a mouse, Willie,
resident of an apartment house wall, links the
lives of two neighboring families in a very unusual way.
[1. Apartment houses—Fiction]   I. Blake,
Quentin.   II. Title.
PZ7.A4384Wi      [Fic]      78-1716
ISBN 0-8038-8086-3

*Printed in the United States of America*

*To Julie, who helped me write it,*
*and to Norman who had just arrived*

# WILLIE
# THE
# SQUOWSE

# 1

Once upon a time on a street in a big city there were two houses back to back.

One house was old and dilapidated, very hot in summer and very cold in winter. The other was newer and well built, very cool in summer and very warm in winter.

Our story begins in the better house, but we will come back later to the dilapidated one so don't forget about it.

In this better house there lived a very nice old couple whose names were Humphrey and Henrietta Pickering. They had been married over thirty years and had one son whose name was Richard.

Mr. and Mrs. Pickering were a very agreeable old couple but they were always worrying. They worried about their son Richard who taught history at a university. Every week Richard sent them an allowance, so they worried that he might lose his job and not be able to send them an allowance. They worried about Richard getting married and then not being able to afford to send them an allowance. They worried about Richard not being able to get married because he had to send them an allowance. They worried when it rained because they were afraid they might catch cold. They also worried when it was hot because they were afraid they might catch sunstroke. Sometimes they worried because they had nothing to worry about.

One day when Henrietta and Humphrey came back from their regular walk around the nearby park they found a large white envelope in their mail box. When they opened it they saw a check for one thousand dollars made out to them by a big stockbroker in the city. There was also a letter. The letter said that the stocks which Mr. and Mrs. Pickering had bought a long, long time ago had suddenly become very valuable. The stockbroker wrote that he would now be sending them one thousand dollars every week and expressed his hope that the stocks would remain valuable forever.

"Do you think it's a good check?" Humphrey asked, his voice barely a whisper.

"There's one way to find out," Henrietta said, looking around to see if anyone could see or hear them.

"How?" Humphrey asked.

"By cashing it," Henrietta replied. Then in a low whisper, spoken near his ear, she said, "Humphrey, get the money in hundred dollar bills."

"Why hundred dollar bills?" Humphrey asked.

"You'll see," said Henrietta. So Humphrey went.

The check was good and Humphrey received ten crisp hundred dollar bills. When he came home Henrietta led him into their neat little kitchen. There, on the kitchen wall, just above the stove, was a hole which Henrietta had made with her bread knife.

"I want to know the money is near us," she explained. "I want to feel it around us. I made this hole in the wall so we can put the money into it each week. We'll cover the hole with a calendar. The wall will be our bank. No one will know."

"That is a wonderful idea," said Humphrey.

Henrietta stuffed the ten hundred dollar bills into the hole in the kitchen wall, and hung a calendar over the hole. Then she took Humphrey's hand and they walked into the living room where they sat down, smiling at each other and sighing happily.

Next week the check for one thousand dollars arrived. Humphrey cashed it and Henrietta put the ten hundred dollar bills into the hole in the wall.

Next week the same.

And the following week the same.

Before long Henrietta and Humphrey forgot they had ever worried about a thing. During their walks around the park they noticed two trees they had never noticed before. They heard music they had never heard before. And most of the neighbors seemed to be very neighborly, which was something else they had never noticed before. They didn't worry when it rained and they didn't worry when the sun shone and sometimes they giggled thinking how silly they had been to worry so much before.

They never bought anything with the money they put into the hole because they didn't need anything. Once Henrietta did buy herself a new pair of knitting needles, and Humphrey bought himself a new clay pipe, but they bought that with the allowance their son Richard still sent them every week. They never touched the hundred dollar bills piling up in their kitchen wall.

And each week the check continued to come. Humphrey cashed it. Henrietta stuffed the bills into the wall. The money grew and grew. The time passed like that happily, and each evening before going to bed they would pray, "God bless all stockbrokers."

# 2

You remember that at the beginning of this story you were told of two houses being back to back. One was the old run-down slum house that was cold in winter and hot in summer. The time has now come to tell you about that house.

In the kitchen of this slum house two men were talking. One man was called Joe. He was short. The other man was called Pete. He was tall. Joe, the short one, was an animal trainer. Pete, the tall one, was a theatrical agent. Pete's job was to find actors and sell them to theaters to do their acts.

Every time Joe, the short one, would start to say something, Pete, the tall one, would shake his head and interrupt, saying, "I know, Joe, but it won't go!"

"Why don't you give me a chance to finish what I have to say?" Joe asked.

"What diffence will it make?" Pete answered. "It just isn't box office. Can't you see it isn't commercial?"

"But I tell you . . . " Joe started to say.

Pete was losing his patience. "Look, Joe," he said, "an elephant, a seal, a dog, even a cat, but not a mouse, Joe. *Not a mouse!*" Pete's voice became loud.

"He is *not* a mouse!" Joe replied impatiently. "He is a *squowse*! His father was a squirrel and his mother was a mouse! That makes him a squowse."

"It looks like a mouse!" Pete insisted.

"He has the face of a mouse," said Joe, "and the tail of a squirrel. He's got the best features of both parents!"

"It still looks like a *mouse*!" Pete shouted, "and I don't like *mice*!"

"You don't have to shout," Joe said. "I've been training all kinds of animals for years and I tell you that this animal is almost human."

Pete tried to hide his exasperation. "I know, Joe, but it won't go!" he said again.

As they were talking, a little brown creature, with brown fur and brown eyes, was doing tricks on a trapeze. He did double flips. He swung back and forth with each paw. He stood on the trapeze with one leg. He got off the trapeze and walked up and back like a soldier. Then he held out his two front legs, hummed *Alouette* and danced a jig.

"See?" Joe said.

"I see," Pete said, "and I hear," Pete said, "but *it isn't box office!*"

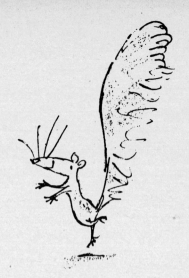

Then the squowse did his best trick of all, giving it everything he had, doing five and a half turns in one somersault and landing on his right front leg.

"His name is Willie," said Joe proudly.

"I can get acrobats a dime a dozen," said Pete.

"But *not* a squowse!" Joe shouted, in total frustration.

Pete got up from his chair, grabbed his hat and said, "I've got to go, Joe. Sorry. The women would scream. There'd be a panic in the theater. No manager would risk it. An elephant act, a dog act, a seal act, even a cat act, but not a squowse act, Joe. It just isn't box office. Can't you see?"

"I tell you Willie is almost human," Joe said, holding Pete's arm. "He understands everything. He can do almost anything. I bought him from a farmer who trained him. It happens once in a million years, something like Willie."

"Maybe so," said Pete, "but I don't go for a squowse act. Sorry."

During all this time Willie was still standing on his right front leg, looking from Joe to Pete and from Pete to Joe.

Pete got to the door and left without saying goodbye.

Willie got down on his four legs and sighed.

"Well, you heard it," Joe said, sitting down and holding his head in his hand.

Willie nodded.

"What's the use?" Joe was still holding his head. He was very depressed. "What's the use about anything?

Maybe it would've been better if you'd had no brains and no understanding and were just an ordinary animal like all the other animals. Maybe it'd be better if you lived like all the others."

Willie felt awful.

"There's no use fooling ourselves," Joe sighed. "I thought our act would sweep the country. I saw you in tails and me in tails, our names in lights, the world at our feet. Pete's right. I was a fool to think a squowse act would go over."

Willie felt worse.

"Anyway, let's get some sleep," Joe said. "We've got to get out of here tomorrow. Let's get some sleep. Perhaps I'll think of something."

That night, while Joe slept, Willie paced the floor. He couldn't sleep. He walked up and back, up and back, and he thought, "What's so terrible? So we don't go on the stage. So we don't get famous. So we're not box office. Is that so terrible? We've got along before. Is that all I've meant to Joe—just a means of getting famous and rich?"

These thoughts troubled him. Willie lay down but he couldn't fall asleep. He started walking up and back again. He was thinking very hard. Then he noticed a little hole in the wall, just above the floor. He stuck his head through. The inside of the wall looked very interesting. Plaster. Lattices. Sticks. Pipes. He scrambled through the hole and started to explore, in the hope that it would take his mind off his troubles. But he was still so absorbed with his thoughts that he didn't look where he was going and slipped. As he slipped a piece of loose plaster fell, hit him on the head, just above the ear, a very soft spot, and knocked him unconscious.

When Joe awoke next morning and started to pack there was no sign of Willie. Joe called him. There was no answer. "Come on now, Willie, I'm not in the mood for games," Joe said. "We've got to get out of here by noon because other people are moving in."

Willie still didn't answer.

"That Willie." Joe was irritated. "Always playing hide and seek. Willie!" he shouted. "Enough!"

Still no sign of Willie. Joe got down on his hands and knees and began looking under the stove, the bed, the chairs and then he noticed the hole in the wall.

"Willie?" he called.

No answer.

Again, "Willie?"

All was quiet.

"He's gone!" Joe said to himself. "He listened to what I said. He's gone to live like all the others."

Joe stood up and braced himself. "It's probably for the best," he said. "Maybe he'll be happier that way. Pete was right. There's no future in a squowse. I'll train an elephant or a seal. I'll miss the little fellow, but if he wasn't box office, what's the use?"

He sighed a deep sigh, waved goodbye and went away.

# 4

When Willie came to, it was the next day. He felt dizzy and he couldn't remember what had happened. Then it all came back to him. "Wonder how long I've been lying here?" he asked himself. "Hope Joe's still asleep."

He made his way carefully through the inside of the wall, looking out this time for falling bits of plaster. He got back to the hole and ran into the kitchen.

The world suddenly became a nightmare. A woman and six children screamed. A man with a red face ran after him with an iron bar. Willie ran under the table. He ran under a chair. He ran under the stove. The man with the red face kept swinging at him and shouting, "I'll get him, don't worry!" The man swung at him again, so hard that he almost made a hole in the floor. "I'll get him," the man kept muttering, as if his whole life depended on his batting Willie's brains out.

"Where's Joe?" Willie kept asking himself, trembling like a leaf. "What's happened to Joe? Can I be in the right place?"

The man with the red face kept poking at him under the stove. "I'll get him," the man vowed. "I'll get him! Don't worry, I'll get him!" The woman and the six children were still screaming. "I'll get him!" the man said again.

"Why?" Willie asked himself. "What have I ever done to them?" He tried to hide further under the stove but the iron bar kept poking at him.

He took a deep breath and made a dash for that hole in the wall. The man missed by a hair. The noise got louder. The woman screamed louder than any of them. "You!" she shouted at the man. "You can't even catch a mouse!"

Willie rushed up the wall, over pipes and wires and sticks and hid in a dark corner, his heart beating fast and loud.

"What people!" he panted. "Barbarians! What kind of world is this that has such people in it?"

He still heard the man saying, "I'll get him, don't worry!" And the woman answering, "You'll get nothing. You've never got anything, and you'll never get anything, not even a mouse!"

They had obviously mistaken Willie for a mouse.

After a few seconds Willie figured out what had happened, that Joe had wakened, found him gone, thought he had run away, and had left without him. Then these savage people had moved in.

"What an unhappy turn of events," Willie lamented, still unable to control his trembling.

Willie lay huddled a long while. Nothing like this had ever happened to him before. Oh, there had been the typical attitude people had when they saw him, but he had become used to it and had forgiven it because he knew it was more out of ignorance than meanness. But no one had ever tried to kill him before. This was a very sad experience. Most people didn't like mice or squice. He knew that. But he had never been attacked before. He had heard about others of his kind being hunted and killed, but until that moment he had felt they had brought it on themselves. Now he felt otherwise. "No one is safe any longer," he thought sadly.

He began to look around to see what kind of place he was in. He walked along a cold water pipe, over some

lattices, jumped on to a wire, and decided that it wasn't too bad a place—if he could provide himself with food.

He kept walking along a pipe until he noticed a large hole in the wall which seemed covered with paper on the other side. He listened and heard nothing. Slowly he pushed his head through the hole and peeked out.

A clean, bright kitchen, everything spick and span, the kitchen of Henrietta and Humphrey Pickering.

At that moment they were taking their regular walk around the park.

Willie was very hungry, and he smelled food, good food. He jumped to the top of the stove and listened.

No sound. He ran to the breadbox, then to the cupboard, took some nuts, a small cracker and ran back through the hole.

"Not bad," he thought, "if I can get food in that nice kitchen every day there's no reason why I shouldn't make this wall my home."

When he finished his meal he began to think about fixing up the place. A little chink in the far wall let in some light. He found a piece of paper, nice and crisp, which made a perfect window shade. There were also old pieces of newspaper which he crumpled up and made

into a comfortable mattress. He found some old string, tied it together and soon had a fine trapeze. Then his sharp ears heard the sound of dripping water. He went to look. There was a leak in a pipe and the water dripped slowly, making a round deep pool. Willie felt the water with his toe. It was just right, so he dived in. He swam around a few moments and came out feeling quite refreshed. Then he looked at his new home, heaved a happy sigh and thought, "Perfect. Everything I need, including a swimming pool."

That night Willie slept peacefully.

When he awoke he felt good. He dived into the pool for his morning swim. Then he did a few turns on the trapeze, which took the place of his morning setting-up exercises, and went into Mrs. Pickering's kitchen for breakfast. Again Henrietta and Humphrey were out for their morning walk and Willie ate his fill.

## 6

So the hours passed into pleasant days and into happier weeks. Willie thought of Joe very often but he didn't feel too lonely because he was so interested in what went on behind those walls—behind the walls of the well-built house and behind the walls of the slum house.

He enjoyed listening to Henrietta and Humphrey when they talked to each other. They were so pleasant. He enjoyed it when their son Richard came to visit, because he knew that made them very happy. He liked the Pickerings very much for what they were, and also because their kitchen was always well stocked. He also liked the regular way they took their walks which made it a simple matter for him to get his food.

Once or twice he thought it might be nice to introduce himself, but that experience with the man with the iron bar had made him extremely sensitive about meeting new people, even if they were as pleasant as the Pickerings. He knew, too, of course, that the old woman, Henrietta, had a strange habit of stuffing crisp pieces of paper into the hole in the wall once every week. It piled up higher and higher, week after week, into a huge mountain. Sometimes Willie rolled around in it, but most of the time he paid it no attention. He reckoned that the hole must be Mrs. Pickering's own private disposal center for her crisp pieces of paper. They were handy as window shades, but beyond that he saw no use for them.

He also got to know the miserable people who lived in the slum house. The man with the red face who had tried to kill him with the iron bar was called John Smith. His wife's name was Mary. The oldest child, Lucille, was fourteen, and the youngest was a boy named Malcolm, about one and a half years old. The children were always dirty. Their noses were always running. All of them sniffed and coughed and kept catching colds. Their mother was

about forty years old, but she looked nearer sixty. She was as sloppy as her children. She never said a pleasant word to them. No one said a pleasant word to anyone in that family. When the father wasn't beating his wife he was beating some of his children and when he wasn't doing that he was asleep snoring. He was drunk most of the time and he hardly ever worked. His wife took in washing to earn a few dollars for food, and was always complaining about her aching back. There wasn't even quiet in this house during the night because the children had nightmares and kept screaming in their sleep. The family was as mean and miserable and unhappy a group of people as ever lived, from little Malcolm, who was always crying, up to the parents, who were always shouting and fighting.

"Very unfortunate people," thought Willie who, by this time, had begun to pity them a little.

## 7

One day while Willie was happily swinging back and forth on his trapeze humming *Alouette* (he knew other songs but he liked that one best), the sudden strong odor of cheese almost knocked him off his swing.

It came from the hole in the kitchen of the slum house. The smell was very strong. Willie gasped for breath.

"They're trying to get me back there so they can knock my brains out," he said to himself. "Well, they won't!"

He tried to bury his nose in his mattress to keep away

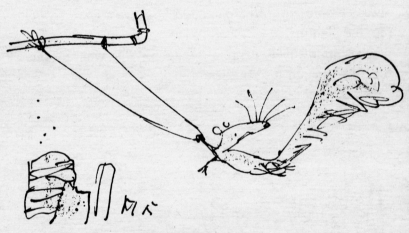

the smell, but that didn't help. It became stronger and stronger. Willie found himself moving toward the hole. He realized that if he didn't do something fast the cheese would draw him through that hole and he'd be caught. He was gasping for breath. He was choking. And he was still moving towards that hole.

On the other side of the wall Mrs. Mary Smith sat on a chair with a piece of cheese in her hand. Mrs. Smith wanted to catch that mouse with the strange-looking tail. She wanted to show her husband that she could catch that mouse, and he couldn't. She wanted to show her husband that he was no good, and she was going to prove it by catching that mouse. She placed the cheese on the floor and got up to get the mousetrap. She heard her children biting, fighting and shouting in the front room so she went to pull them away from each other, slapping faces right and left.

Willie, meanwhile, was being driven out of his wits by the smell of that cheese lying near the hole. He made a quick dive into his pool and swam under water as long as he could but he had to keep coming up for air and the smell hit him each time.

Then an idea came to him and he knew that he was saved.

"I've got to plug up that hole with something!"

Breathlessly he rushed to the pile of crumpled paper,

grabbed one, scampered down the wall without making a sound, and quickly plugged the hole.

He took a deep breath and sighed with relief.

There was no more smell of cheese.

Mrs. Smith, in the meantime, returned to her kitchen, picked up the mousetrap, sat down on the chair and bent down to pick up the cheese. Then she noticed that the hole in the wall was plugged with something.

"Now that's funny," said Mary Smith who was sure the hole had been empty a few moments before. She looked closer. She took a fork, got down on her knees and pulled at the paper. When she straightened it out she found herself looking at a hundred dollar bill.

For a full sixty seconds Mary Smith stared at that hundred dollars. She then looked back at the hole. Then she picked up the piece of cheese and looked at that. Then she sat down and stared at the hundred dollar bill again.

"It's a dream!" she whispered to herself.

The piece of cheese dropped from her hand. Within three seconds the hole was filled again. Mary Smith rushed to close the kitchen door, rushed back, picked up the cheese and then pulled out what was filling that hole.

Another hundred dollar bill.

She prayed. She asked forgiveness for all her sins. She

promised to be a good woman, a good wife, a good mother. She promised to live all the days of her life in righteousness. She promised to be patient, humble, forgiving, loving, unselfish, brave, noble, and a pal and a buddy to her children.

Then she dropped the cheese again and waited.

Within a few seconds the hole was plugged again—but with a piece of plaster.

Willie hadn't had time to go back for the paper to stuff the hole.

Mrs. Smith prayed again. "I know," she whispered, "I was too greedy. It only works twice. Not three times. Please give me another chance tomorrow."

She took the plaster from the hole, put the cheese back in her refrigerator and hid the two hundred dollar bills in her bosom.

Willie sniffed, smelled no cheese, grinned to himself, thinking, "They've given up," and went back to his trapeze.

That night Willie slept well, but Mrs. Smith didn't. She was waiting for next day. And next day, at exactly the same time, she walked into her kitchen, quietly locked the kitchen door, carefully took the cheese from her cupboard and gingerly placed it near the hole in the wall.

She waited.

Nothing happened.

"Perhaps I didn't do it right this time," she said, biting her lip nervously.

She tried to do everything exactly as she had done it the day before. She sat down in the same place, put the cheese down in the same spot, got up to get the mouse-trap, even walked to the front room and slapped all her children.

But the hole remained empty.

The hole remained empty simply because Willie was in Mrs. Pickering's kitchen eating breakfast. The smell of the cheese didn't carry as far as Mrs. Pickering's kitchen. Willie finished his meal—and started to return to his dwelling place.

At that instant Mrs. Smith saw that she was not sitting on the same chair! On the day before she had been sitting on an old broken-down chair with no back. She got that old chair and sat down and dropped the cheese—and it happened!

Another hundred dollar bill filled the hole.

Mary Smith almost fainted from excitement. "I've got the secret! *The chair! The old chair!*" she whispered to herself, almost crazy with joy.

She took the hundred dollar bill from the hole, sat down on the old chair again, dropped the cheese, and the hole was filled again.

This time she could barely control herself. When she took the second hundred dollar bill her hands shook. She put the cheese away and tried to think about the miracle that was happening in her kitchen.

"Twice a day, no more, no less," she mumbled to herself, in a hushed voice.

In the meantime, Willie was rushing back to plug the hole a third time with another piece of crisp paper. He stopped and sniffed. No smell of cheese. "Maybe they realize they can't catch me that way," he thought, very satisfied with himself.

Next day Mrs. Smith quietly led her husband into the kitchen. "What do you want?" he asked gruffly.

"You've got to see it to believe it," she said, "but once you've seen it you must promise not to tell a soul. God has answered our prayers. We're rich."

"Have you been drinking?" asked Mr. Smith in a suspicious voice.

"No," answered his wife. "Now watch," she said as she took a piece of cheese and pulled up the old chair and sat down.

"The poor woman has gone off her head," thought Mr. Smith.

He saw his wife drop the cheese. He saw her smile.

Then he saw her bend down and take something from the hole in the wall. She gave it to him. It was a hundred dollar bill.

Mr. Smith didn't say anything. His wife was still smiling. "See?" she said. "Now the hole is empty." Mr. Smith looked. Yes, the hole *was* empty.

"Now," said his wife, sitting down on the chair and dropping the cheese again, "now watch."

The hole was no longer empty.

This time Mr. Smith got down on his hands and knees and pulled out the piece of paper.

"How?" he finally managed to say, unable to believe what his eyes were seeing.

"It's the old chair," his wife whispered. "That's the secret."

Mr. Smith looked at the old chair, and then looked at his wife, and then at the hundred dollar bill and then at the hole. He couldn't figure it out.

"It works twice a day," his wife explained. "No more, no less. It happened two days ago. I didn't want to tell you about it before I was sure it would work again. Every day we get two hundred dollars. At the end of a week we get fourteen hundred. At the end of a month we get six thousand dollars!"

"And we don't have to pay any taxes on it," said Mr. Smith.

"Yes," Mary Smith giggled.

"How do you know it only works twice a day?" Mr. Smith asked.

"I tried it three times and a piece of plaster was put there," she answered.

"But how . . . ?" Mr. Smith began again.

"The Lord works in mysterious ways," said his wife. "It is not for us to question."

"Maybe we should tear down the wall and see what's behind it?" said Mr. Smith.

"If you do you'll find nothing and the miracle will stop. This is how we must do it. The old chair, a piece of cheese, twice a day, no more, no less. If we're too greedy we'll get nothing," his wife cautioned.

"I still can't believe it," said Mr. Smith.

"We'll try it again tomorrow and you'll see," said his wife.

Willie was very disappointed about having to keep on worrying about his safety.

Next day came the familiar smell of cheese.

Willie filled the hole and stopped the smell.

The piece of paper was taken away and there was the cheese smell again.

Willie filled the hole a second time.

The paper was taken away and there was the smell of cheese *a third time*!

By now Willie was really fed up. He ran up the wall and peeked into the Pickering kitchen. As luck would have it they were out taking a walk. "I'll hide in their kitchen until that terrible smell goes away. If the Pickerings come home, I'll just have to go back and stuff that hole again," thought Willie.

On the other side of the wall Mr. Smith was shaking his head, staring into the empty hole.

"I told you!" shouted Mrs. Smith angrily. "It only works twice! No more, and no less!"

"It *is* a miracle," whispered Mr. Smith.

"Why don't you listen to me sometimes?" asked Mrs. Smith.

"I will," said her husband. "I will. From now on I'll listen to everything you say."

Mrs. Smith picked up the cheese from the floor and triumphantly led her husband from the kitchen.

Willie poked his head back into the wall and sniffed. No smell of cheese. "They've given up," he thought, jumping back into the wall.

But next day the smell of cheese came again.

Willie filled the hole once.

The paper was taken away and there was the smell of cheese a second time.

Willie filled the hole twice.

The paper was taken away—*and this time there was no more smell of cheese.*

"All right," thought Willie, accepting the challenge. "All right! if that's the game they want to play, *all right!*"

And so each day he plugged the hole twice, and each day Mr. and Mrs. Smith went through their ritual, and each week Humphrey cashed the check and Henrietta kept stuffing the hundred dollar bills into the hole of her kitchen wall.

And that was how the wall Willie lived in became a sort of bank and Willie a sort of banker.

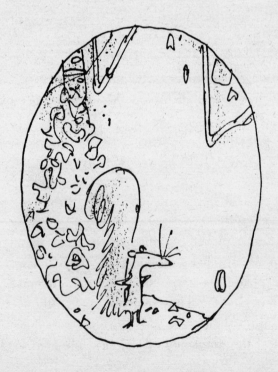

# 8

The weeks thus passed into eventful months, eventful months into significant years until some five epic-filled years had passed.

The Smith children were no longer dirty. They were neatly dressed, clean, and well-mannered in the presence of strangers. Their noses didn't run and they stopped catching colds. Lucille became a pretty, if affected, young woman of nineteen, and went to college. The Smiths now owned their house and had had it completely renovated. It was now warm in winter and cool in summer. There was new furniture, a grand piano on which all the childred practiced, a telephone with two extensions, a double-sized refrigerator, a stereo, an electric washing machine and drier, a maid and two cars.

Mr. Smith still drank as much as ever but no one seemed to mind any more. All the neighbors took off their hats now when he passed. Whenever something happened anywhere in the world they would ask him to explain it and Mr. Smith always had explanations. And all the neighbors remarked at how Mr. Smith had changed from a loutish drunkard into a prosperous, charming and witty *bon vivant.*

When a newspaper reporter asked him what was the secret of his success, Mr. Smith puffed on his cigar and answered, "Hard work and taking advantage of opportunity when it knocked."

The reporter wrote it all down. "That," said Mr. Smith, "is responsible for my being where I am today. But if the real truth were told . . ."

"Yes?" said the reporter who was going to write Mr. Smith's life story for a big newspaper.

"If the real truth were told," continued Mr. Smith, "I'd have to say I owe everything to my wife."

"You are a very modest man," said the reporter.

"You can also add that as another reason for my success—modesty," hiccuped Mr. Smith.

Mrs. Smith had also become famous in her own right. Almost every other day the society pages of the newspapers reported what she wore, where she went, what she did and what she said. She went to teas, gave money to charity, christened two battleships, and began to ride horses, which is something people in big cities often do when they get rich.

As the Smith children grew older they wanted to move from their house to a classier neighborhood but their parents wouldn't hear of it. "This is where we achieved our success, and this is where we'll stay," they said loyally.

The children could understand their parents' sentimental attachment to the old house but they couldn't understand why they refused to part with that old broken-down kitchen chair that had no back.

"It's an eyesore," the children said.

"It's a family heirloom," Mrs. Smith explained, "and it means a lot to us."

The children teased them about it, and their rich friends snickered at their attachment to the ugly old chair, but Mr. and Mrs. Smith didn't mind that.

9

You've probably been wondering whatever happened to Willie's former friend, Joe, during all this time. I have hesitated telling you, because this part of the story is not very pleasant, but I'd better get to it now.

Soon after leaving Willie, Joe got everything in his life he ever thought he wanted. He trained an elephant (using hypnosis) to wear petticoats and dance the can-can, while

playing a trumpet with her trunk, none of which the elephant enjoyed doing. The act proved to be a howling box office success and soon Joe owned a large troupe of half-dazed dancing and trumpet-blowing elephants who were featured in a Hollywood musical film purporting to dramatize the love life of elephants. It was a travesty both of love and of elephants. The film earned its producers a fortune and Joe became a rich and powerful man in show business.

But Joe had enough conscience to be ashamed of himself because the once-proud elephants were humiliated by their act. He got no satisfaction from the money which came from exploiting unhappy elephants hypnotized into wearing petticoats, kicking up their legs and blowing trumpets.

He gradually realized that from the time he had left Willie, he had not experienced one true moment of joy in his work. He had never made a real friend. This state of affairs could only lead in one direction—downwards.

He became addicted to alcohol, besotting his brain, so he wouldn't have to think about anything and would be able to forget Willie, the best friend he'd ever had. He became the easy victim of a gang of unscrupulous businessmen who stole his elephants and then all his money in shady business undertakings. When last heard of, he was slithering fast down the road to ruin—to loneliness, starvation and painful isolation.

We shall have to leave him in this sad state for the moment, and return to the Smiths and the Pickerings.

## 10

Now, the college Lucille Smith attended was the same college, naturally, that Professor Richard Pickering taught at. Naturally they fell in love. And naturally, when he proposed, she accepted.

Lucille brought Richard home to meet her family. He liked the Smiths and the Smiths liked him.

"It's time there was a professor in the family," said Mrs. Smith.

Richard brought Lucille to meet his parents and Henrietta and Humphrey approved the instant they learned she was the daughter of one of the wealthiest families in the land.

"She's a complete dear," said Henrietta.

"She is that," said Humphrey.

Lucille told Richard how wonderful she thought his parents were. Richard said, "Yes, they have something I've always admired. It came rather late in their years, but they've had it ever since—a love for people, a sense of belonging to a good world, a patient and wise understanding of human weakness."

"My parents have that too," Lucille said thoughtfully.

"Some people have it," Richard said, "and some people haven't."

# 11

The day came when a letter arrived from the stockbroker telling Henrietta and Humphrey that the enclosed check was the last one, that the stocks were of no value any longer and that he was happy to have served them all this time.

Humphrey cashed the check. Henrietta put the hundred dollar bills into the hole in her kitchen wall and smiled a secret smile.

"We have enough money," she whispered to Humphrey.

"More than enough," he answered in his pleasant, quavering voice.

"You know," Henrietta said, "money isn't as important as some people think it is."

"That is so," said Humphrey.

Henrietta and Humphrey walked into their front room and sat down on their sofa, holding hands, as they had done for so many, many years. They were content and they were very old. They closed their eyes knowing that their time had come. They died peacefully and blissfully, their hands still clasped together.

When Richard heard of his parents' death he felt very sorry, but he knew they had lived a long and secure life. He knew their time had come and that they had died peacefully and securely, which was all they'd ever wanted out of life. He never knew about the money, and even if he had, it wouldn't have mattered to him by then.

When Henrietta and Humphrey Pickering were laid in their final resting places, Willie found himself without food. The kitchen was bare. The supply of food Willie had packed away in his wall lasted only a few weeks. Then he began to get hungry.

The hungrier he got the dizzier he got when he smelled that piece of cheese from the Smiths' kitchen. He kept filling the hole twice each day, but every time he approached it he had to control himself so as not to rush through and grab the cheese. The morning came when the pile of crisp paper was all gone. It was also the morning when the temptation of that cheese smell became unbearable.

Hunger began to overcome fear. He decided to take a chance.

Mrs. Smith sat on the old chair she had sat on every morning for over five years. The piece of cheese lay in front of her.

Willie's little head poked its way carefully through the hole.

His curiosity got the better of him. Instead of grabbing the cheese and running, he looked up and for a second his eyes met the eyes of Mrs. Smith.

She let out a piercing scream, picked up her skirts and jumped on the chair. The old chair gave way under her, collapsed, and everything fell in one heap on the floor.

Willie grabbed the cheese and scampered back through the hole as fast as he could—back to his bed, his trapeze and his swimming pool.

Mrs. Smith's screams brought her husband running into the kitchen. He helped her to her feet. When she looked at the broken chair she wept bitter tears. "That funny-looking *mouse!*" she cried. "If it weren't for that miserable little mouse I wouldn't have broken our magic chair."

Mr. Smith said, "Now let us not be hasty. Let's try it without the chair and see what happens."

He placed another piece of cheese near the hole. Willie was happily munching the big piece of cheese he had captured and paid no attention.

Mr. Smith waited and nothing happened. "It *was* the old chair, after all," he said.

Mrs. Smith suddenly felt generous about the whole thing. "We've been getting it now for five years. Perhaps it's someone else's turn?" she said.

"I suppose that's right," said Mr. Smith. "Besides, we don't need it any more. The properties we now own make us a hundred times more money than we'll ever need."

And so the Smiths moved. They began another life in a new neighborhood and before long Mr. Smith ran for Congress and was elected.

When the Smith family left, their house remained empty.
The Pickering house remained empty. One day some men
came into the kitchen of the old Smith house and Willie
heard them talking about tearing it down as well as the
Pickering house, as well as a lot of other houses nearby
to make room for a big new office building. Willie knew
that the time had come to leave and find a new home.

He traveled light. There was nothing much he had to pack
because he knew he could make himself at home wherever
he went. But he did take his trapeze and he did take his
window shade. It was a good window shade and it was
the last piece of crisp paper left in the wall. He had for-
gotten all about it until he started to leave. He crumpled
the paper into a ball and tied his trapeze around it, leaving a piece of string to hold on to. He reckoned that the

paper might come in handy some day, either as a shade or as something to plug up a hole if the occasion arose.

So Willie threw his belongings over his shoulder and left his home in the wall. He reached the sidewalk and sniffed the cool air. Willie hadn't realized it was winter. There was snow on the ground. He heard church bells ringing and the music of Christmas carols. It was Christmas Eve.

The streets were lonely because most people were at home celebrating. Willie heaved a sigh and started down the street when he noticed the feet of a man standing on the sidewalk. They seemed familiar. Willie looked up at the man's face.

The man was very sad. His clothes were in rags. His shoes were torn. He looked hungry. The man stared at Willie and his sad face broke into a big happy smile. "*Willie!*" he shouted, joyously.

Willie almost cried, he was so happy. The man, of course, was Joe.

"Willie, Willie," Joe whispered, bending down to caress Willie's head. "It's been so lonely without you. I reached what I thought was the top and it was worse than the bottom. I lost my self-respect, and became the nothing you see now."

Willie tried to make Joe feel better by rubbing against his hand to remind him they were together again.

"For the last couple of years," Joe said, "I've been coming back to this street hoping to find you, but never really believing I would. Willie, will you ever forgive me for being such a fool?"

Willie just kept rubbing his head happily against Joe's hand. Of course he forgave Joe everything.

Then Joe noticed the piece of paper Willie was carrying. "It's a miracle!" Joe cried out. "A Christmas miracle! May I have it, Will?"

Willie nodded, and wondered why that piece of paper made Joe so happy. He wondered why those pieces of paper had made the Smiths and the Pickerings so happy. "I suppose," thought Willie, "that these pieces of paper make humans happy. It must be the way of the world."

Joe held the hundred dollars in his hand and said, "We'll get a meal. Then I'll buy some shoes. I'll start again." He looked into Willie's eyes. "I'm going to try and not make the same mistake again," he said. "I'll work only at whatever brings us both joy, and if we ever have to work at a job that isn't any fun, we'll do it only if it doesn't make anyone else unhappy. You agree, Will?"

Willie nodded again. Of course he agreed. He'd always felt that way.

"I know now I'll never be happy unless you're with me," said Joe. "Do you feel the same, Will?"

Willie jumped a backflip and did three somersaults to show Joe how pleased he was. Joe laughed and Willie jumped into his pocket. Then Joe walked proudly down the street and the bells were ringing happy sounds. And both Willie and Joe knew that from that day on they would live happily ever after.

It is quite possible that one of these days you may meet a happy man who is traveling with a squowse. Hum *Alouette* to the squowse. If he hums it back and dances a jig you'll know for sure that it's Willie.